THE ADVENTURES OF MARITIME DOMAIN AWARENESS MAN

THIS GRAPHIC NOVEL IS DEDICATED TO THE OCEANS AND TO ALL THE PEOPLE

WORKING TO KEEP THEIR MAGIC AND WONDER ALIVE

BY NICK TOMB

DESIGN AND ILLUSTRATION BY LETI ARTS, ACCRA, GHANA

IN SCHOOL

AFTER SCHOOL

HOME

Go down to the wharf and help your father...

HAND ME THOSE NETS, KOFI.

PAPA, I WANT TO GO OUT TO SEA WITH YOU!

NO! YOU HAVE TO STAY HERE AND COMPLETE YOUR SCHOOLING

BUT I WANT TO GO! I WANT TO HELP EARN MONEY TO SUPPORT THE FAMILY!

NO!

IN OTHER NEWS, TODAY THE GOVERNMENT LAUNCHED A PROGRAM CALLED THE SECURITY GOVERNANCE INITIATIVE, DESIGNED TO ENHANCE MARITIME DOMAIN AWARENESS (MDA) IN THE GULF OF GUINEA.

MARITIME DOMAIN AWARENESS IS AN UNDERSTANDING OF WHAT'S IN AND WHAT'S HAPPENING IN A NATION'S OCEAN. UNDER THE UNITED NATIONS CONVENTION ON THE LAW OF THE SEA

A NATION HAS TERRITORIAL WATERS THAT GO 12 MILES OUT FROM SHORE AND AN EXCLUSIVE ECONOMIC ZONE (EEZ) THAT GOES 200 MILES OUT TO SEA. ALL OF THE RESOURCES--LIKE FISH, OIL AND MINERALS-- IN THIS ZONE BELONG TO THE NATION, AND OTHER NATIONS MUST PAY TO USE THEM.

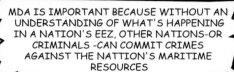

MDA IS IMPORTANT BECAUSE WITHOUT AN UNDERSTANDING OF WHAT'S HAPPENING IN A NATION'S EEZ, OTHER NATIONS-OR CRIMINALS -CAN COMMIT CRIMES AGAINST THE NATTION'S MARITIME RESOURCES

WE LOSE HUNDREDS OF MILLIONS OF DOLLARS IN ILLEGAL, UNDER-REPORTED FISHING THAT OTHER COUNTRIES TAKE FROM OUR EEZ EVERY YEAR.

WE HOPE THAT BY KNOWING WHAT OCEAN RESOURCES WE HAVE AND KEEPING THEM FOR OUR OWN USE, WE'LL GENERATE THE FUNDS WE NEED TO PROTECT OUR MARITIME DOMAIN. IN OTHER NEWS, THE AFRICAN WORLD CUP KICKED OFF IN SENEGAL WITH MALI PLAYING...

DON'T WORRY MOM, I'LL FIND A WAY TO MAKE SOME MONEY!

SIGH... YOU'RE A GOOD BOY, KOFI. WE'LL FIGURE THIS OUT. HOPEFULLY YOUR FATHER GETS A GOOD CATCH!

HAVE TO FEED THE BABY!!

OIL SPILL!!

PIRACY!!

NO FUTURE!!

PLASTIC POLLUTION!!

THE CRIMINAL GANG THAT'S BEEN ATTACKING LOCAL FISHERMEN STRUCK AGAIN LAST NIGHT, ROBBING A LOCAL FISHING VESSEL OF ITS ENTIRE FIVE-DAY CATCH, THE THIRD REPORTED ROBBERY THIS MONTH.

HEY, KOFI, WHATCHA DOING?

OH, HI ESI, NOT MUCH, JUST HEADING HOME FROM SCHOOL.

I HAVEN'T SEEN YOU AROUND LATELY. I THOUGHT WE WERE GOING TO WORK ON MY NEW DRONE.

YEAH, I'M SORRY, I'VE JUST BEEN BUSY TRYING TO HELP MY MOM WITH MY BROTHER AND SISTER. MY DAD HAS BEEN OUT FISHING A LOT LATELY

MY DAD SAID, IT'S GOTTEN REALLY DANGEREOUS OUT AT SEA WITH THAT CRIMINAL GANG ATTACKING SO MANY LOCAL FISHERMEN...

...YOU SHOULD REALLY HELP ME WITH THE DRONE. I'M ALMOST DONE WITH CONSTRUCTION. MY DAD SAYS IF WE KNOW WHAT'S GOING ON OUT AT SEA, WE CAN PROTECT OUR LOCAL FISHERMEN.

WELL, YOUR DAD IS THE COMMODORE. I GUESS HE WOULD KNOW!

WELL, HERE'S MY HOUSE. WHY DON'T YOU COME IN AND HELP ME FINISH UP?

UH, OK... IS YOUR DAD HOME? HE ALWAYS KIND OF SCARES ME!!!

DON'T BE SILLY, HE ACTUALLY REALLY LIKES YOU!

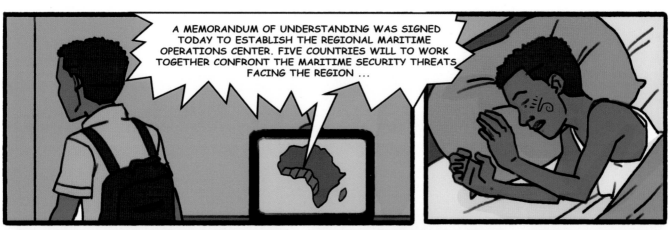

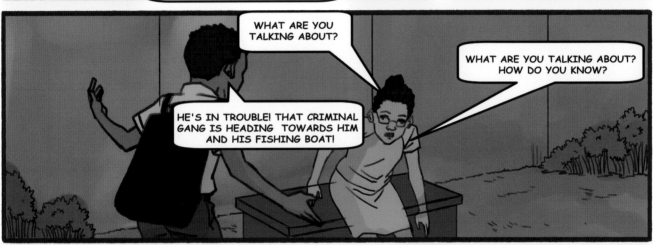

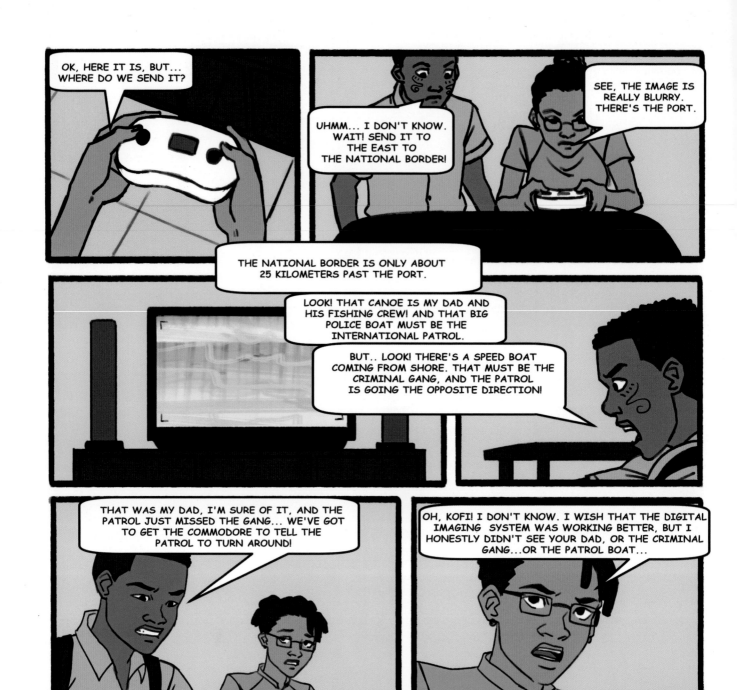

KNOCK
KNOCK

COME IN!

HI, HONEY! OH, HELLO KOFI.

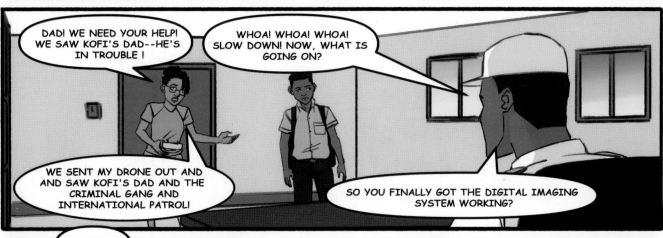

DAD! WE NEED YOUR HELP! WE SAW KOFI'S DAD--HE'S IN TROUBLE !

WHOA! WHOA! WHOA! SLOW DOWN! NOW, WHAT IS GOING ON?

WE SENT MY DRONE OUT AND AND SAW KOFI'S DAD AND THE CRIMINAL GANG AND INTERNATIONAL PATROL!

SO YOU FINALLY GOT THE DIGITAL IMAGING SYSTEM WORKING?

WELL... KINDA...

DO YOU HAVE A PICTURE YOU CAN SHOW ME?

SIR, ESI'S DRONE WAS WORKING GREAT. WE WERE JUST PAST THE PORT WHEN WE SAW MY DAD'S FISHING CANOE. IT WAS HEADING WEST. WE ALSO SAW THE INTERNATIONAL PATROL, WHICH WAS HEADING EAST. IT WAS ABOUT 15 KILOMETERS FROM THE BORDER.

THEN WE SAW A SPEED BOAT TAKE OFF FROM SHORE, JUST AFTER THE PATROL PASSED. IT WAS HEADING WEST, AFTER MY DAD. IT MUST HAVE BEEN THE CRIMINAL GANG!. THEN THE SYSTEM WENT DOWN AND THE SCREEN WENT OFF.

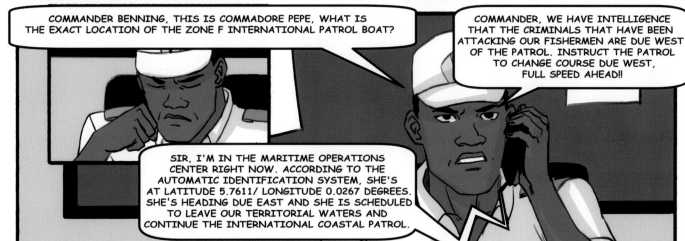

COMMANDER BENNING, THIS IS COMMODORE PEPE, WHAT IS THE EXACT LOCATION OF THE ZONE F INTERNATIONAL PATROL BOAT?

COMMANDER, WE HAVE INTELLIGENCE THAT THE CRIMINALS THAT HAVE BEEN ATTACKING OUR FISHERMEN ARE DUE WEST OF THE PATROL. INSTRUCT THE PATROL TO CHANGE COURSE DUE WEST, FULL SPEED AHEAD!!

SIR, I'M IN THE MARITIME OPERATIONS CENTER RIGHT NOW. ACCORDING TO THE AUTOMATIC IDENTIFICATION SYSTEM, SHE'S AT LATITUDE 5.7611/ LONGITUDE 0.0267 DEGREES. SHE'S HEADING DUE EAST AND SHE IS SCHEDULED TO LEAVE OUR TERRITORIAL WATERS AND CONTINUE THE INTERNATIONAL COASTAL PATROL.

THREE MEN SUSPECTED TO BE MEMBERS OF THE CRIMINAL GANG, WERE ARRESTED BY A PATROL TODAY JUST OUTSIDE OF THE PORT. THIS ARREST DEMONSTRATES THE CAPABILITY OF THE INTERNATIONAL FORCE AND THE VALUE OF INTERNATIONAL COOPERATION TO ADDRESS SHARED MARITIME SECURITY INTERESTS.

KOFI SAVED HIS FATHER.

HE IS LEARNING TO CONTROL HIS POWERS.

BUT HE IS GOING TO HAVE TO GET A LOT STRONGER TO FACE THE DANGERS AHEAD!

TO BE CONTINUED...

Dear Reader,

Thank you for picking up the first issue of The Adventures of Maritime Domain Awareness Man—I hope that you enjoyed it!

It has been an exciting journey to create this superhero and produce this graphic novel. I look forward to many more adventures with Kofi and Esi, and hope that you will come along for the ride.

Did you know that 70% of the planet is water, that 80% of humans live within 100 miles (160 km) of the ocean, and that 90% of global trade takes place on the waterways? It's true, but it's also true that 100% of humans live on land.

As a result, we often don't think about what is going on over the horizon, out in the ocean. We suffer from "sea blindness." This means that we are not aware of the things that happen there — good or bad. Right now, our oceans are in danger. Pollution, over-fishing, piracy... there are so many threats facing our seas. When we do things like use a plastic straw one time then throw it away and it winds up in the ocean, or when we buy illegally or un-sustainably caught fish, we are contributing to the problem. We are the villains. But we can also be the heroes!

When we don't throw away that plastic straw after one use, or when we buy fish that was sustainably caught, we are helping to solve these problems and make our world a better place.

The Adventures of MDAM is a way to help spread awareness about the oceans, to help everyone understand and care about what is happening in the waters that make up the majority of our planet. Together, with Kofi and Esi, we will explore the many challenges facing our oceans. And we will also look for solutions, ways to protect the seas and the animals that live in them--as well as ways for humans to benefit from all that the maritime domain has to offer in a sustainable, symbiotic way.

I hope that you will join us on this journey,

Nicholas Jomb

PS: Turn the page to find more info and a sneak peak of The Adventures of Maritime Domain tAwareness Man issue #2, which will be available very soon!

TO BE CONTINUED
IN ISSUE 2...

 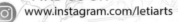